To every kid who dreams about hitting one out of the park,
and to Hank Aaron, who showed us all how to do it with dignity and honor.—M. L.

To my nephew Kevin —D. K.

Text © 2008 by Mike Leonetti.

Illustrations © 2008 by David Kim.

Book design by Mariana Oldenburg.

Typeset in Rockwell.

The illustrations in this book were rendered in acrylic on illustration board.

Manufactured in China.

Library of Congress Cataloging-in-Publication Data

Leonetti, Mike, 1958–

Swinging for the fences : Hank Aaron and me / by Mike Leonetti ; illustrated by David Kim.

p. cm.

Summary: Mark, a young baseball fan, follows Hank Aaron's career as he tries to break
Babe Ruth's all-time home run record. Includes biographical information about the famous baseball player.

Includes bibliographical references.

ISBN 978-0-8118-5662-1

1. Aaron, Hank, 1934– —Juvenile fiction. [1. Aaron, Hank, 1934– —Fiction. 2. Baseball—Fiction.]

I. Kim, David, 1977– ill. II. Title.

PZ7.L5513Sw 2008

[E]—dc22

2007012655

10 9 8 7 6 5 4 3 2 1

Chronicle Books LLC

680 Second Street, San Francisco, California 94107

www.chroniclekids.com

Swinging for the Fences

Hank Aaron and Me

By Mike Leonetti

Illustrated by David Kim

chronicle books · san francisco

"Mark, we just need a hit to tie the game," Coach Parker told me as I went to bat. "Try for a base hit and we can even the score."

I nodded, but what I really wanted to do was hit a home run and win the game.

I took a mighty swing at the first pitch.

"Strike one," yelled the umpire.

The next pitch was on the outside corner of the plate. I managed to get a piece of it, but the ball went foul—strike two.

The next pitch came right over the middle. I watched the ball as it left the pitcher's hand. I could see the stitches on the ball spinning toward me. *I can smack this for an easy homer,* I thought to myself. I ripped another swing and missed it completely!

"Strike three! You're out," barked the ump.

The game was over. We lost 3–2. The coach just looked at me as I walked off with my teammates. I knew what he was thinking. He'd reminded me many times about how I shouldn't always try to hit home runs, but I couldn't help it.

Hank Aaron, the right fielder for the Atlanta Braves, was my hero. Dad told me that Hank might be the best home-run hitter of all time. People said he carried his bat like a hammer and gave him the nickname "Hammerin' Hank." I wanted to play just like him.

By 1973, Hank had hit 673 home runs, more than any other player except Babe Ruth. The Babe had hit 714. I tracked Hank's homers on a poster I had on my wall. Most people thought Hank would break the Babe's record this year. I listened to Hank's games on the radio and watched them on TV whenever I could. I wouldn't go to sleep before I marked my chart with Hank's latest home run.

Every year I bought baseball cards hoping to find one of Hank for my collection. The first pack I bought for the 1973 season had Bobby Bonds of the San Francisco Giants, Vada Pinson of the California Angels, Tim Foli of the Montreal Expos, and Fergie Jenkins of the Chicago Cubs—but no Hank.

The next pack had Ralph Garr of the Braves, Roy White of the New York Yankees, Tony Oliva of the Minnesota Twins, and Jim Palmer of the Baltimore Orioles, but still no Hank. My sister bought me my next pack. I tore into it hopefully and found Willie Horton of the Detroit Tigers, Carl Yastrzemski of the Boston Red Sox, Reggie Jackson of the Oakland A's, Tony Perez of the Cincinnati Reds, Lou Brock of the St. Louis Cardinals, and Willie Stargell of the Pittsburgh Pirates. When I got to the very last card in the pack, I gave my sister a big hug—it was Hank Aaron!

That July, Dad and I went to a Braves home game against the Philadelphia Phillies. I brought my baseball bat to the game for Hank Aaron to sign. At the stadium, Dad bought me a Braves cap with a big *A* on it and a pennant with *BRAVES* written across.

"Do you think Hank will get his 700th home run today, Dad?" I asked as we made our way to our seats.

"He just might. You know, the first time I learned about Hank was from listening to games on the radio. The Braves were in Milwaukee then, and Hank hit the home run that won the Braves the 1957 National League pennant."

"Wow, that was a long time ago," I said. Dad laughed.

"I was only a few years older than you are now, Mark. We watched the '57 World Series on TV at school. The Braves beat the Yankees in seven games, and Hank hit three home runs. Not many people believed in the Braves, but they did it."

"Wouldn't it be great if the Braves made it to the Series again?" I thought out loud. "Maybe we could watch the games on TV at school, too."

In his first at bat, Hank hit a single. When he came to bat for the second time, everyone sensed that he was about to knock one out of the park. He let a couple of pitches pass. Then, on a low pitch, he took an uppercut swing, sending the ball toward the left-center-field stands. It was home run number 700! A billboard in the outfield showed the new mark.

As Hank rounded the bases, the Braves fans gave him a standing ovation. He tipped his cap high in the air. I was so happy to be there, I didn't even mind that the Phillies beat the Braves 8–4. Now, if I could get Hank to sign my bat!

"**M**aybe he's not coming out this way, Mark," Dad said as we waited at the players' exit. Everyone else had gone, and there was no one around.

"Just five more minutes, please Dad," I pleaded.

Then, there he was—my hero, Hank Aaron. My hands were sweating, and I gripped my bat very tightly. My heart raced.

"Go ahead, Mark. Ask him," Dad said, nudging me forward.

Hank noticed me, saw how nervous I was, and smiled. Finally, I was able to speak.

"M-Mr. Aaron, could you sign my bat please?"

"Sure. What's your name?"

"My name is Mark, sir. I'm on a baseball team too, and whenever I'm at bat, I always try to hit a home run, just like you."

"Sounds like you're quite a player," Mr. Aaron said.

"Well," I said, blushing a little, "I don't always hit the ball. A lot of times I strike out."

"You know, Mark, I didn't start out trying to hit homers. It just sort of happened over time."

"Really?" I asked in amazement.

"Sure. When I was coming up, I just wanted to be in the major leagues. For the first six or seven years of my career, I hit more doubles than home runs, and I really concentrated on getting as many RBIs as possible. I did what I could to help my team win."

"You sound like my coach and dad, Mr. Aaron," I said.

"There are different ways to succeed in baseball, Mark. Players who hit singles, steal bases, and play well in the field are just as important as home-run hitters. I take great pride in doing what the team needs. Your team is counting on you to help them win, so listen to your coach. He knows what the team needs from you, OK?"

"I'll try, Mr. Aaron," I replied. "I sure hope you break Babe Ruth's record," I added.

"Thanks for the encouragement, Mark. Breaking the Babe's record would be nice, but I want people to remember me as a good all-around ballplayer too," Hank said.

While my dad and Hank spoke for a
few minutes, I looked at Hank's autograph.
Someday, maybe people would ask for mine.

For the rest of the season, I watched Hank chase Babe Ruth's home-run record. He hit 40 home runs, but ended up one short of tying the record. The Braves didn't make it to the play-offs, but my team did. Unfortunately, we didn't get too far. I was still swinging for the fences and missing the ball too often.

Just before Christmas, I got a package in the mail. When I saw the return address was from the Atlanta Braves, I tore it open. Inside was a book by Hank Aaron called *Hitting the Aaron Way: Baseball's Greatest Home-Run Hitter Teaches Youngsters to Hit*. Inside the cover was a note:

Dear Mark,

It was nice to meet you over the summer. Here is a new book I just completed that might be helpful to you. I want to thank you for your good wishes and support. Young fans like you make me want to live up to expectations.

Most sincerely,

Hank Aaron

I'm going to read this cover to cover, I thought.

Hank's book was full of good advice: Be ready to attack the ball when you step up to the plate. Develop a hitting style all your own. Swing hard, but control the bat. Just making good contact with the ball is enough; home runs will come when you have the power to hit them. And finally, Hank said that practice was important for everyone because everything could be improved.

As soon as it was spring, Dad and I went to the diamond near our house and started tossing the ball around. I practiced hitting and fielding, and Dad gave me some good pointers he remembered from when he played baseball.

At long last, the new baseball season began. The Braves started the season with three away games in Cincinnati. Dad and I watched the first game on TV and listened to the others on the radio.

In his first at bat of the season, Hank cranked out a three-run homer. He had tied the Babe's record! I hoped Hank wouldn't hit another home run until the Braves were back home Monday night. Dad and I had tickets to that game, and I wanted to see him break the Babe's record in person.

Monday morning it rained. By game time it was cloudy and chilly, but the rain had stopped. Dad and I got to the stadium early so we wouldn't miss anything. We bought a program with a picture of Hank on the cover.

As Hank stepped up to the plate for the first time, it started to drizzle. I couldn't believe I was watching this game! Was Hank about to hit his record-breaking homer? Dodgers pitcher Al Downing didn't give Hank anything good to hit. Hank took a walk and later scored a run when his teammate Dusty Baker hit a double. That was exciting, but over 53,000 fans wanted to see Hank knock one out of the park.

Hank was up again in the fourth inning. The crowd rose to its feet as he put his hard hat over his soft cap and stepped into the batter's box. This was it—I could feel it!

Downing's first pitch was in the dirt. I gripped Dad's shoulder and stood on my toes. The second pitch came toward the center of the plate. Hank took his usual smooth swing and made a strong connection.

SMACK!

The ball sailed over the head of shortstop Bill Russell and kept rising, heading toward left center field. My heart was pounding! The Dodgers outfielder, Bill Buckner, tried to climb the fence, but the ball was gone. It cleared the sign on the outfield fence that read "385 feet," and ended up in the Braves bull pen.

"YES!" I yelled. "HOME RUN!"

Hank Aaron had broken the Babe's record!

The crowd exploded with shouts and thunderous applause. We stayed on our feet and cheered the new home-run champion. Our faces were lit up like the center scoreboard that flashed 715. Fireworks went off in the outfield. Hank's smile was so huge, Dad and I could see it from where we sat. Braves pitcher Tom House brought the ball in from the bull pen. After he tagged home, Hank took it and lifted it up so the fans could see.

Not everyone wanted this day to come. Some people didn't want a black man to break Babe Ruth's record. They even wrote Hank terrible letters and threatened his life. I didn't understand why people would do that, but none of it mattered now. It seemed that none of those awful people were in the stadium tonight.

ATLANTA SALUTES
Hank Aaron

Dad boosted me onto his shoulders so I could see better. "This is a great night, Dad," I said.

"It is," Dad said. "Hank worked really hard to get here."

"I'll always remember this," I said.

Hank stepped to a microphone on the field and told the crowd he was happy that the chase for the home-run record was all over. When he finished speaking, the game continued and the Braves won 7–4.

My own baseball season began about a month after Hank hit his record-breaking homer. I wore number 44 on my jersey in honor of my hero.

In the very first game, I came to the plate with the bases loaded. It was our last at bat—we had two outs, and we were down by two runs. I had already struck out twice.

"Alright, Mark," said Coach Parker. "A good solid hit will score two runs and maybe even get us the lead. Just try to make good contact and drive the ball."

I nodded and stepped up to the plate. For just a second, I thought about hitting a grand slam. Then I remembered Hank's advice. I watched the pitcher closely. When he threw a ball straight down the middle, I said to myself, *Just make solid contact.* I watched the ball and . . . WHACK!

The ball rocketed between the center and right fielders. Everyone was running hard. I made it to second base and all our runners scored! We won the game 4–3. It felt great to help my team, just like Hank Aaron said it would.

"Nice hit, Mark."

"Thanks, Coach Parker. I think our team is going to have a great year."

About HANK AARON

ATLANTA OUTFIELD
HANK AARON BRAVES

Hank Aaron was born on February 5, 1934 in Mobile, Alabama. His mother, Estella, was very important to him. She often told Hank to try to be the best at whatever he did and to strive to achieve his goals.

She knew Hank needed an education to do that, and wasn't happy at first when Hank preferred to play baseball. However she saw how much Hank loved baseball and agreed to let him play for a local team for $10 a game, as long as he continued to study.

Hank was such a good player that in 1951 he was offered his first professional contract. At the time, African American players could only play in the Negro Leagues, a baseball circuit made up of teams with only African American players. Hank played for the Indianapolis Clowns.

In 1947, when Jackie Robinson, Aaron's boyhood idol, became the first African American to play in major-league baseball, the Negro Leagues began to fade away. In fact, in 1952, when the Boston Braves, a major-league team, bought Hank's contract, he became the last major-league player to come up from the Negro Leagues. He made his major-league debut in 1954. By that time, the Braves had moved to Milwaukee.

Hank had an amazing major-league career right from the start. In 1956, he hit .328 and won the National League batting title. In 1957, he was named the most valuable player of the National League and won his only

World Series title. He went on to hit 30 or more home runs a season 15 times during his career, and 40 or more home runs eight seasons of his career. He managed to hit .300 or more a total of 14 times over the course of his career. By the time his career was over, he had hit a major-league-record 755 home runs and 2,297 runs batted in (RBIs). His most memorable hit came on April 8, 1974, while a member of the Atlanta Braves, when he clubbed his 715th career home run, passing Babe Ruth as the all-time leader.

Hank's 3,771 career hits, 3,298 games played, and 2,174 runs scored rank him third all-time in each category. He was very proficient in the field. As a right fielder, he took the Gold Glove, an award given for outstanding individual performance in the field for three consecutive years—1958, 1959, and 1960.

Hank Aaron retired in 1976, after appearing in more than 20 All-Star Games. He was inducted to the Baseball Hall of Fame in 1982. In retirement he became an executive with the Atlanta Braves, and is currently the vice president of player development.

On August 7, 2007, San Francisco Giants outfielder Barry Bonds hit his 756th career home run to break the all-time record held by Aaron. While he was not at the game, Aaron offered his congratulations to Bonds in a video that was broadcast at the stadium right after Bonds broke the record.

"I would like to offer my congratulations to Barry Bonds on becoming baseball's career home-run leader. It is a great accomplishment which required skill, longevity, and determination," Aaron said.

"Throughout the past century, the home run has held a special place in baseball, and I have been privileged to hold this record for 33 of those years. I move over now and offer my best wishes to Barry and his family on this historic achievement. My hope today, as it was on that April evening in 1974, is that the achievement of this record will inspire others to chase their own dreams."

SOURCES

The author referred to the following sources while researching this story:

Books

Aaron, Hank (with Lonnie Wheeler). *If I Had a Hammer: The Hank Aaron Story,* Harper-Collins Publishers, New York, 1991.

Aaron, Hank (with Joel Cohen). *Hitting the Aaron Way: Baseball's Greatest Home-Run Hitter Teaches Youngsters to Hit,* Prentice-Hall Inc., New Jersey, 1974.

Canfield, Jack (ed). *Chicken Soup for the Sports Fan Soul,* Heath Communications Inc., Deerfield Beech, Florida, 2000.

Golenbock, Peter. *Hank Aaron: Brave in Every Way,* Harcourt Inc., New York, 2001.

Plimpton, George. *Hank Aaron: One for the Record,* Bantam Books, New York, 1974.

Stanton, Tom. *Hank Aaron and the Home Run That Changed America,* Harper-Collins Publishers, New York, 2004.

Tolan, Sandy. *Me and Hank,* Simon and Schuster, New York, 2000.

Magazines

Braves Scorebook 1974, Atlanta Braves, 1974.

Hank Aaron Press, Radio and TV Guide, published by the Atlanta Braves, 1973.

Sports Illustrated, April 15, 1974 issue, story by Ron Fimrite.

Articles

"Hank Aaron Memories," in *Limelight,* Gemstone Publishing Inc., April 29, 2005.

"Hank Aaron: Still the Hitter of Record," by Larry Stone, *Seattle Times,* May 7, 2006.

"Hank Aaron's Story," by Michael Aun, as it appeared on www.aunline.com, 2004.

"Interview with Hank Aaron," by Bryan Ethier, *American History Magazine,* June, 1999.

"Home Run Chat with Long Ball Legends," in *Baseball Digest,* Evanston, Illinois, June 2006 issue.

Our Record, by Royce Webb, SportsJones.com, April 8, 1999.

"The Hammer Weathered a Pounding as Ruth Loomed," by Ron Kroichick, *San Francisco Chronicle,* May 9, 2006.

Remarks by President Bill Clinton at Hank Aaron gala held in Atlanta, Georgia, February 5, 1999.

"Sports Heroes: Hank Aaron," by Justin (surname not given) from Fredericksburg on www. SportsHeroes.com, undated.

Video

Greatest Sports Legends: Baseball: The Modern Era, Hank Aaron 1954–1976, Marathon Music and Video, Eugene, Oregon.

Hank Aaron: Chasing the Dream, produced by TBS Productions Inc., Atlanta, 1995.

Web sites

BaseballLibrary.com

Wikipedia.org